HEIST AT DAWN

SARAH BIJO JOHNS

Published by wordU, India

info@wordu.in
www.wordu.in

Heist At Dawn

A wordU Book/ published by arrangement with the author

ISBN: 978-93-47985-08-9

Typeset and Cover Design by Cogitabund LLP
Printed and bounded in India by Manipal Technologies Limited

MIX
Paper | Supporting responsible forestry
FSC® C043100

wordU Private Limited is committed to a sustainable future of our business, our readers and our planet. This book is made from Forest Stewardship Council® certified paper

Contents

HEIST AT DAWN

SARAH BIJO JOHNS

word

The Characters

--- The siblings:

- Jess (The oldest),
- Victor,
- Michael.
- Doris (The youngest)

--- The gang:

- Pedro
- James
- Arthur

--- Pedro's Grandfather:

- The old man

Short Summary

This book is a mystery-solving book for young and lively readers. It's basically how four ordinary siblings solve a mystery, symbolising their courage and bravery throughout the story. With unexpected twists and turns, ups and downs, and betrayal, this book creates fantasy and thrilling suspense in the mind of the reader. Moving to the rest of the story, these clever detectives learn the hard way when one of their new but close friends betrays them. But that was not the end for the four. Read every page to discover what happens next...

Acknowledgement

A Great Amount Of Thankfulness For Those Who Contributed To This Book.

1. First of all, I would like to thank Jesus for all His blessings in my life.

2. Secondly, I want to thank my family for being with me throughout the entire journey of book writing. Without your opinions and cooperation, writing this book would not have been possible.

3. I would also like to say a heartfelt thank you to the principal and teachers of Sanskara School for creating this challenge to boost our writing skills and for allowing us to write and publish a book.

Acknowledgement

Chapter 1
JESS AND HER SIBLINGS

In the beautiful suburbs of Chrilstone, there stood a cottage, lonely and out of sight. Cobblestones lined its pathway, and numerous ivy vines twisted here and there, giving it an enchanting look. But there wasn't anything truly enchanting about the house. In fact, it was quite old, and in it lived a girl named Jess and her siblings—Victor, Michael, and Doris—a group of four who loved detecting and were detectives themselves. They were a bunch of teens, with Doris being the youngest at thirteen.

The four loved exploring, discovering, and inventing things. They were always eager to try something new and were full of enthusiasm. It was half past seven in the morning, and their sleep was disturbed by Victor's alarm. He sat up, rubbing his eyes, still sleepy. He looked to the side and saw his brother Michael still fast asleep at the edge of the bed. "Wake up, Michael," Victor said, shaking him to get him to open his eyes. Then he took his water bottle and sprinkled some water on Michael's face. Michael woke up with a start.

"Good morning, Victor," he said. "Are Doris and Jess awake?"

"No, not yet." Just as Victor said that, he heard a knock at the door. He went to open it. Doris stood there with tea for both of them.

"Hey," said Doris as she walked in with the tea. "Thanks," said Michael and Victor together.

"Well then, I'm going back to my room with Jess for more sleep. You two better call me when it's eight o'clock." Saying this, she left the room and went back to where Jess was sleeping.

An hour later, Jess woke up to a knock at the door. "It's half past eight, Doris!" exclaimed Victor, throwing a soft pillow at her. She woke up, quite annoyed, and threw one back at him.

A few minutes later, they all went downstairs for breakfast. Victor and Jess baked cranberry scones, while Michael and Doris made the orange sauce for dipping. Once everything was ready, they sat at the table to eat.

"I'm quite glad our parents are on vacation; we can do what we like!" said Victor. "Yes, it's a pleasure," Jess said.

"Most importantly, there are no rules. We don't have to hear 'Stop that!' or 'Go to bed!' anymore," said Victor. In a while, they finished their breakfast and went to wash the dishes. Michael finished first, and then he sat on the couch, thinking. His siblings joined him.

"You look quite confused, Michael. What are you thinking about?" asked Doris.

"You know," Michael went on, "what if we go camping this week?"

"Mum and Dad usually don't let us," said Victor. "Well, we could ask," Doris replied.

So, they called their parents on the telephone.

"Hey Mom, are you free?" Jess asked. "Yes, Jess, tell me," her mother replied.

"What do you think about the four of us going camping on Chrilstone Hill?"

There was a minute of silence.

"Alright, your dad agrees too," Jess's mother said. "Thank you, Mom," she said back.

Then she remembered.

"Mum, how is your and Dad's trip to Hawaii?"

"Oh, very well indeed! The only thing is, the food here is much different from in Chrilstone."

"Well, it is Hawaii after all. Bye, Mom, I need to go."

Saying that, she ended the call.

"Let's go camping then," she said. They couldn't wait, and they were hoping for a shrill of mystery in the air.

Soon after, they decided what to pack. Doris jotted it

down on a piece of paper: torch, tents, map, sleeping bags, binoculars, candles, and packed food. She went to the kitchen to pin it on the fridge so that she would remember to pack everything.

It was 1 p.m., so Michael went to make ham and sausage sandwiches, and Victor, Doris, and Jess made some salad and pasta.

They ate their lunch and then had guacamole afterwards because their big appetites were still not satisfied.

When it was nearing five, they went for a cycle ride. It was a cool day, with carnations, lavenders, and poppies growing in the fields. The wheels of the bicycles rattled against the cobblestones, and they could hear sparrows singing. There wasn't anyone in this lonely place, just insects and flowers to ponder. Nearby, there was a wood with a lovely creek and many flowers growing there too.

That was when the breeze turned cold and the clouds grew darker. It started to shower, and a few raindrops fell on Victor.

"It's getting quite dark; we should head back," came Victor's voice.

So, they turned to go.

In an hour, they reached home, back at the cottage. They rested their bicycles and went inside. They had returned at the right time, for it had already started raining heavily.

Right away, they began preparing dinner. They made steak covered with mushroom sauce, with mashed potatoes, vegetables such as broccoli, carrots, and beans, and two pieces of garlic bread as side dishes. After they had finished eating dinner, they went to their rooms, excited for tomorrow.

"Goodnight, Jess."

"Goodnight," she said back. "Wake up early tomorrow, Doris. Be ready for the big day."

Who knew, there might be a mystery waiting for them, and they might be the detectives, just as they had always longed to be.

Chapter 2
THE BIG DAY

It was six in the morning. The weather was calm now, and they could see raindrops on the windows and dewdrops on the plants. The sun had come out, and there was a beautiful rainbow.

Victor's alarm rang at half past six. He went to brush his teeth and made sure that he had packed everything. Then he went to wake Michael up. Victor, however, had to remind him several times where they were about to go, because Michael had nearly forgotten about the camping trip, even though it was his idea.

"Looks like the girls haven't woken up yet. Let's call them," Victor said. So he went downstairs with Michael to their room and opened the door.

"Doris, Jess, wake up!" he said. They woke up. "What time is it?" Jess asked, startled.

"It's about seven now," Michael said.

This made the girls alert, and they did everything in a rush. In a few minutes, they were dressed, had brushed their teeth, and, referring to the checklist Doris had made, ensured that everything was packed. They carried their bags and, using a rope, attached and tightened them to the backs of their bicycles. The wheels had been pumped with plenty of air the day before.

"So, are we ready to go?" Doris asked. "Yes, I suppose so," said Victor.

After everything was double-checked, they darted down the hill on their bicycles and followed the route just as the map guided them. They had a mini race. Jess was the fastest of all and won the race with her unwavering speed.

When they were halfway there, they stopped cycling when they saw a pastry shop. Next to it was a coffee and tea shop. They first entered the pastry shop. The doorbell clattered.

"Two Nutella croissants and two plain ones, please," Jess asked the server.

"Would you like something else, like a beverage?"

"No thanks," said Michael.

They started eating the croissants in a hurry, and Jess began hiccupping.

"Shoot!" she said, embarrassed.

After they finished, they went to buy something from the coffee and tea shop. They looked around the shop. The main theme was gold and white, and it looked brand-new.

They had so many types of coffee to choose from: latte, cappuccino, iced, warm, French, Indian, and regular. It also had a wide variety of teas, including black, green, and normal tea.

"Two regular teas, one latte, and one French coffee, please," Jess said to the server. In about two minutes, she brought the drinks to the table.

"That was quite quick," Doris said. The server then handed them a packet of chips.

"It's on the house," she said.

"Well, that's nice," said Jess. "How much should we pay you?"

"Four pounds in total," the server said. Michael tipped an extra pound to the lady. After they had finished their coffee, they went to their bicycles and got on.

The map said that Chrilstone Hill was after three more sharp right turns and a broad left. After two right turns, they came to a cherry blossom orchard, with

light pink flowers falling from the trees. "How many turns are left?" Michael asked. "About two more," Doris replied.

"Is that Chrilstone Hill over there?" asked Victor. "Seems like it," Jess answered. The moment the four had been waiting for had finally come.

They started cycling up the steep hill and reached the top at last. It had a crooked and wide peak, but the view was exquisite and unimaginable— like something out of an enchanted movie. They noticed a "PROHIBITED AREA" surrounded by wires.

"What a view," said Victor. And when he turned around to see the sign, he felt it was out of place. He wondered why the sign was there.

They started putting up their tents and unpacking their heavy bags. They organized things in each corner of the tent. The tents were huge but only fit two people, so Doris and Jess set up another tent for themselves. They also set up a barbecue outside so that they could roast food.

As it was nearing lunchtime for them, the four started eating eggs on toast with marmalade, which they had packed, along with drinks. While eating, the girls came from their tent to eat with the boys in theirs, so they were all together.

They sat down on the mat to eat. "No parents, no rules, and most importantly, we don't need to do chores!" exclaimed Jess. In half an hour, they were done with lunch.

"Let's see, the map says there's a butterfly garden here, just a few kilometres away," said Doris.

"Why don't we go there?" she asked.

"Why not?" Victor said. And so the four turned to go.

They came to the butterfly garden. "Pedro's Rare Butterfly Species" was written on the greenhouse.

"Where's the owner?" asked Michael. An old man appeared from an old brick chimney house.

"Hey, lads," he said. "Came to see my garden?"

"Yes, sir. It would be great if you gave us a tour— all of us, especially Doris, as she loves spotting rare butterflies," said Victor. The old man led them to the greenhouse.

"At first glance, your eye catches the beautiful wings of the purple emperor and the Menaulus blue morpho butterfly, two very rare species found in England and Mexico, respectively. Then," he said, "you can spot some magnificent orange monarch butterflies. They love sucking nectar from coneflower and milkweed flowers, and they live about nine months. They're found largely in the United States or the continent of Australia," he went on.

At the end of the tour, they got to see the glasswing butterfly. Its transparency made it look unique. After they were done, they turned to leave. But before they could, they met the old man's grandson, Pedro, who was about their age.

"Oh, so they both live here," said Michael to himself. They had a chat with him and then turned to go. The four thanked the old man, said goodbye, and headed back to their tent.

When they reached their tent, they started eating dinner. They sat on the mat, which was set up on the grass, allowing the four to enjoy nature. Michael unpacked a few sausages and ham sandwiches for everyone, and they began eating. They finished their dinner quickly and got ready in their pyjamas to go to bed early, as they were already tired. It was nine o'clock, and the siblings said their goodnights to each other.

Before they went to sleep, they didn't forget to call their parents on their cell phones. Then the four zipped themselves into their sleeping bags.

"Goodnight, you three," said Jess. "Goodnight!" they said back.

Chapter 3
GETTING TO KNOW PEDRO

The alarm rang. It was nine in the morning. Jess woke up first, yawning. She shook Doris, and eventually she woke up too.

"Good morning, Jess," said Doris. "Good morning," she said back. "Have the boys gotten up?"

"No, let's go wake them up," Jess said. They went to Michael's and Victor's tent and woke them up. They brushed their teeth, changed out of their pyjamas into fresh clothes, and went to eat breakfast, in which they had bacon, eggs, and French toast, Jess's favourite and secret recipe.

"It looks like a king's feast," Victor said.

"It does," agreed Michael. "Let's eat quickly. I want to see the butterfly garden again," Doris said.

After they finished breakfast, they went on their bicycles to the butterfly garden. It was ten minutes past ten now, and the sky looked bright and clear. As always, a few kilometres ahead, they saw a glimpse of the butterfly garden. The old man was watering the plants in his garden, and Pedro was looking after the kittens and dogs.

"Hey, nice to catch up with you again," Pedro said to the four.

"Want me to give you a tour around the house and take

you to our farm?"

"A farm? That'd be amazing!" Jess said.

As they were walking, Pedro asked them, "So, have you come here for a trip?"

"Actually, we came here for camping. It's our holidays," Victor said. They went around the farm and saw many animals—a pig called Henry, who was just about four years old. The four played around with him. They saw cows, dogs, and kittens, too, until they came to a peculiar, colourful-looking bird that flew to Pedro's shoulder.

"What species of bird is that?" asked Michael.

"Oh, that's a parakeet, and his name is Panny," answered Pedro. After they finished the farm tour, they went into the old man's home.

The house was white, with stains on it. It rose to the height of a large cottage and had windows all around. It was old, and the floorboards creaked as you stepped on them. As they looked, a big, old mechanical clock on the wall in front of them fascinated the four. After spending some time there, they went upstairs to see some rooms on the second floor. After they explored about half of the rooms in the whole house, they were called for tea.

"We should perhaps go," said Doris after some time. "No, please stay. I insist," said the old man.

So, the four stayed and had snacks with them. To their astonishment, there were twenty croissants and ten cream buns. They wondered who had baked all of these. There was tea and coffee too. They knew they could not eat lunch anymore. "This coffee is derived from 1887, and was collected by Pedro's great-great- great-great-grandfather and..." And before the old man completed his sentence, Pedro whispered, "one of his usual lectures again."

Michael laughed. "But he's jolly good and funny as well," he said.

"Yes, I couldn't agree more," Pedro said. No one talked as they ate, so Michael asked, "Sir, did you make all this?"

"Yes, I did. I used to be a cook, and still am," he said. In twenty minutes, they finished the tea, and Pedro took them to the last floor of the house. As they came to the last room, they noticed a large, dark black case.

"What's in there?" Jess asked and went to open it. "Wait, don't open that!" shouted Pedro, and it frightened Jess out of her wits.

"Sorry, Jess. That case is precious and not to be opened."

"Alright," she said, wondering why her friend Pedro got

so angry when he seemed so nice at first.

In a while, they finished and prepared to return to their tents. They waved back at Pedro and his grandfather and went back.

Half an hour later, after cycling through cobblestone roads, they reached their tents. It was half past twelve now, and they started preparing lunch for themselves. They unpacked some food for them to eat. Accompanied by those dishes, there was a fruit drink for each of them as well.

It was a lot to eat, so they only finished after a while.

After lunch, they had their juice and started reading some books.

"I'll be checking the map for more places to visit and explore, since we love doing that," said Victor. "Good idea. I'll join you too," Doris said.

The map said there was a crystal lake about five miles away. "Let's go there tomorrow."

"That's far, but let's go there," Doris said.

After looking at the map, they also found a cave they could visit, which was just a mile away.

"Well, that's a lot of places, so we'll visit one place at a time," Michael said.

"All I want now is a glint of mystery to solve. We've always been keen on solving them, but have never actually gotten one to solve," Victor said.

"You're right, I've been waiting for one too, but let's not lose hope. Who knows, there might—just might— be a mystery awaiting us," said Doris.

At about half past seven, the sun started to set.

"Oh, look at the sunset," Jess said. The sky was orangish-red, and there were faint pink clouds. The sun itself was an eye-catching crimson red colour. It seemed to sink behind the other Chrilstone hills, for there was not just one hill but many. They viewed the gleaming sun with their binoculars. Everyone took a turn.

After viewing the sunset, they went back inside.

It was nearing night now. The sky was turning a dark black colour. The trees between the hills seemed to whisper, and the faint, pink full moon had just come out from behind the pine trees, where it had been hiding. Not long after, their stomachs started to grumble.

"It's getting late, and we should start eating dinner," Michael said. He unpacked some burgers and took out the jar of cut fruits. The four shared the fruits and finished quickly. They were in a state of excitement for the coming day, since they would be visiting a lot of places.

"Why don't we watch the stars today?" Victor said. "Let's go outside," Doris said. They saw constellations like the Big Dipper (also known as Ursa Major) and many shapes in the sky. They also saw the full moon shining directly onto their faces. The stars were near the moon, and the scene felt like it was straight from an enchanted movie. It was nearing ten p.m. already.

"Let's go inside now, shall we?" Jess asked, and so they went inside.

They changed into their pyjamas and were ready to sleep.

"Goodnight!" Doris said.

This time, to say a sweet goodnight, it was their parents who called.

"Goodnight, Mum, and goodnight, Dad," they said and went to sleep. Victor and Michael fell asleep. Though Jess and Doris kept turning side to side, they couldn't sleep, and their hearts were beating with excitement. They could not stop thinking about how much fun they were going to have tomorrow. All of them were excited, such that they could not stop tossing and turning in their sleeping bags. They weren't wrong, though! They would have the best day.

Chapter 4
OFF TO CHRILSTONE LAKE

It was half past nine in the morning, and Victor's alarm rang. He woke up. He unzipped a bit of the tent because he heard raindrops. He shook Michael to wake him up.

"Michael!" he said. "Wake up!" Michael woke up. "What?" he asked. "Why do you look worried,

Victor?"

"It's raining, and we ought to reach Crystal Lake by half past ten," he said.

"That's in about two hours," Michael said, and almost went back to sleep.

"Two hours? We barely have an hour left," Victor spoke again. This made Michael quickly unzip his sleeping bag.

Good thing they had packed an umbrella just in case. Victor, holding the umbrella, went to the other tent to wake the others up.

Yes, they had only thought about an umbrella a few minutes before they started from home.

"Jess, Doris, get up," he said. They woke up. "Oh, hey, Victor. What's the time? It's early, I suppose,"

Doris said.

"Early? It's just fifteen more minutes to ten a.m.!" he

exclaimed. The girls got up, and Victor went back to his tent. To everyone's relief, the rain stopped soon after, when all of them were ready to go.

"Let me check the directions on the map again," Jess said. "Two right turns and two sharp left turns, and then straight. There's a stream nearby, too," she said.

The four quickly ate two grilled cheese sandwiches each in Jess's and Doris's tent, took some water bottles, and, in case they got hungry, stuffed some candies in a bag and took four scones to eat. They jumped on their bicycles and sped down the hill. The clouds were quite bright now, with dandelions swaying in the wind in a valley. Doris plucked some, as she was fond of dandelions, even though they were considered weeds. She never understood why.

As they were nearing the lake, the clouds grew light grey.

"We should reach there in about ten minutes," Victor said loudly, for there was faint thunder in the sky.

"Terrible weather today," Michael replied.

Just as they were losing hope, they got a glimpse of sunlight. They were almost there, but when they saw a clear stream, they went to drink from it with their hands. They took a look at the beautiful landscape. Crows were flying in the air, and the valley was full of fresh grass, which swayed from side to side, as if they were dancing and welcoming them. After they were done, they hopped back on their bicycles and started pedalling quickly.

Just as they were losing hope, they got a glimpse of sunlight. They were almost there, but when they saw a clear stream, they went to drink from it with their hands. They took a look at the beautiful landscape. Crows were flying in the air, and the valley was full of fresh grass swaying from side to side, as if dancing and welcoming them. After they were done, they hopped back on their bicycles and started pedalling quickly.

It was eleven a.m. when they reached. They had to walk for a while until they saw the lake, shimmering and light blue in colour. Above it was a high cliff with a rope attached to the end.

"The lake looks good and clear," said Jess. "Why don't we first climb the cliff and then dive into the water from there?"

"Sounds dangerous to me," said Michael.

"It's a big lake, and there's no risk in doing so," Jess said.

"Alright, let's do it then. But first test the rope before you try climbing it," Victor said.

The rope was strong and durable. Doris climbed first,

then Jess, Victor, and then Michael. After they reached the end of the rope, they held the edge of the cliff with their hands and crawled up.

Good thing they wore shoes; there were many sharp rocks and cliffs. Once all of them reached the top, they saw fields, hills, and valleys in front of them, covered with fog. They went on to explore the cliff. While exploring, they spotted some pebbles and weeds.

"Nothing much here," Jess said. "Let's go back." They were getting ready to dive.

"Great idea of yours, Victor, to wear our swimsuits under our clothes," said Doris.

The four gathered at the end of the cliff, ready to jump. "Three, two, one—jump!" said Jess.

After they were done, they did it again. They also swam together and had races. When they got tired, they rested. They had brought a few towels to dry themselves.

After all that swimming, they felt hungry. "I'll unpack the candies and scones," said Michael. They chatted while they ate. After they were done, they packed everything back into a bag and headed toward their tents. It was already half past three now, and the four had enjoyed themselves in the last few hours.

It was nearing half past four when they arrived at their tents at last. Once they went into their tents, they changed their clothes quickly.

The sun was setting, and it was evening now. The four read books. They had brought a device to watch movies on.

Jess made some popcorn. Michael and Victor watched *The Chronicles of Narnia*, and Doris and Jess watched *Bridge to Terabithia*. They couldn't finish the whole movie since it was nearing dinnertime, but they planned on watching it while eating dinner.

The four unpacked some mac 'n' cheese and did not eat much, for they were already half full. This time, Jess and Doris went to the boys' tent to eat. They took their device to watch the movie along with Victor and Michael.

It took more than half an hour for the four to finish the movies they were watching. When they were done, the girls said goodnights to Victor and Michael and returned to their tent. They did not forget to call their mum and dad. So did Victor and Michael.

"Goodnight, Mom. Goodnight, Dad," they said. "We'll be visiting a cave tomorrow," Doris said.

"Oh, that's great, but be cautious and look out for sharp rocks," Mrs Charlotte, their mother, said, and hung up the call.

"Goodnight, Michael," said Victor. "Goodnight," he said back.

The girls also said their goodnights to each other. Jess set an alarm to ring at half past six a.m., so that this time all of them could wake up earlier for tomorrow.

Jess closed her eyes and zipped her sleeping bag. She fell asleep quickly. But Doris kept tossing and moving in her sleeping bag, full of excitement. But in a while, she too fell fast asleep. By that time, it was raining. Michael woke up, freezing, but cuddled back into his sleeping bag.

It was morning. The alarm was going to ring in about ten minutes. Thankfully, the weather was sunny, even though it had rained the night before. The grass on the hill was wet, and it was foggy.

The alarm rang. Doris was the first to wake up. She woke up Jess. While in the boys' tent, Victor got up first. He woke up Michael.

"Good morning," he said.

"Is it still raining?" Michael asked.

"No, the sun's out, and the weather is good today," Victor said. "We need to go to the cave today, remember?"

Michael and Victor ate some biscuits and jam muffins. Doris and Jess ate some toast and cream buns. They had a fruit drink at the end. They were ready to go.

Chapter 5
EXPLORING THE CAVE

"So, are we ready to go to the cave? Did we pack our lunch?" asked Victor.

"Yes, we packed everything, and our bicycles' wheels are still in shape. Let's start our journey then," Doris said.

They started cycling down the hill at top speed. When they reached the bottom of the steep hill, they came across the croissant and coffee shop they had stopped at when they arrived. As they were cycling, Michael asked, "Why don't we stop at Pedro's butterfly garden today, before we reach the cave? I would like to see him again."

"Yes, we can. We'll spend some time in his house,"

Doris said.

They cycled up to the butterfly garden. No one was outside.

"Sir?" Jess shouted, trying to call the old man. He came out of his house.

"You four again! Come in," the man said. While they were in the house, Jess asked where Pedro was.

"Oh, he's gone off with his friend somewhere, like usual," he said.

"Do you know where he went, sir?" Doris asked. "Oh, he won't tell me, no matter how many times I ask him. I don't know what he's up to these days." "Well, we came to see him. Just tell him that. We must go to the cave now, sir. Have a good day!" said Victor.

"Are you talking about Chrilstone Cave? I've heard stories about precious objects being looted or stolen and hidden there. But children, carry on—there's nothing to be afraid of," the old man assured them. They waved goodbye and went on their bicycles.

"Valuables being hidden there? What does he mean?" Michael asked.

"I don't really know, but as he said, there's nothing to worry about. We're just being paranoid," Jess said. They had cycled for a very long time, and all four of them gotvery tired indeed.

"Let's take a break; my legs hurt," Doris said. As they saw a stall selling caps, they went and bought four— one for each of them—since it was sunny.

After they took a break, they saw the cave in the distance. They rested their bicycles near a mulberry bush and went inside the cave.

"It looks dark. Do you have a torch, Victor?" Michael asked.

"Oh yes, I forgot. I'll switch it on," he said. "Fascinating," Jes s said, looking at the cave. After walking for a while, in front of them, they saw a pathway divided into three paths.

"Which one should we go through?" Doris asked.

Victor looked at the map.

"These pathways lead to different places, but have an exit at the end anyway. Let's go through the second one;

it's a shortcut," he said. As they went on walking, the cave became too narrow to fit through, and the four had to crouch since the roof was growing lower. They started to feel uncomfortable.

"We should have chosen either the first or the last path," Michael said.

"You're right," Doris said.

As they went on again, in front of them were two pathways.

"Guess we'll choose the first one," Jess said. As they were walking along the first path, they noticed a strange metal door on the side. It wouldn't budge even an inch.

"What's this for?" she asked.

"I don't know," Victor said. "It really is an unusual place to keep a door."

"Yes, it won't move no matter what, and what a complex door lock!" Michael said.

"How strange it was for a huge metal door to be fixed in a random spot in the cave," the siblings wondered. Leaving that aside, Jess, Doris, Michael, and Victor started pacing forward until they came to a dead end. They were puzzled.

"Huh, we must have followed the wrong path. Let's go back," Doris said.

"But we did exactly like the map said," replied Victor.

It was strange.

The siblings, with their torches shining brightly, walked in the opposite direction. The way along this path was not very low, and the four got just enough space to fit through.

Just a while later, they came to the door they had stumbled upon earlier. After they came back outside, the sun was shining brightly, with rays falling directly on the four. The sunlight was mottled on the forest floor. The daisies and bushes near the cave moved from side to side, as if saying goodbye to them.

The four hopped on their bicycles and sped up the hill, passing Pedro's butterfly garden along the way. "What do you think about Pedro?" Victor asked. "Well, he's quite nice," Jess said.

Little did they know, the person they thought would be loyal might betray them, shifting the story's perspective unexpectedly. Soon, they reached their tents at the top of the hill.

By the time they arrived, it was a quarter to one, and the four were desperate for food. They unpacked their lunch, laid a mat outside the tent, and began eating while enjoying the view of the countryside from the hill. Their peaceful meal was interrupted by a crow that snatched a couple of French fries. In half an hour, they were finished. They packed everything up and went into their tents.

Bored with reading, they played UNO and Monopoly for entertainment. Jess excelled, winning every single game, but her siblings kept trying without giving up.

After finishing, they took a pocket-sized map neatly folded into Victor's pocket.

"About 10 miles away, there's a museum named 'Antique Collections, since 1985'," Victor said.

"That doesn't seem bad to visit," he added.

"Isn't that a far distance to cover by bike?" Jess asked. "You're right, but some exercise will be good,"

Michael replied. So, they made up their minds to visit the museum the following day.

"There are a lot of marvellous places to visit in a countryside with a scanty population," Doris said.

"Yes, we've visited many places, and we got a tiny hint of mystery to sense when we found that metal door in the cave," Michael said. The four loved mysteries and were eagerly waiting for them. They had grown up watching detective movies and aimed to be detectives someday.

A few hours later, Victor's stopwatch rang. It was 7 p.m. already! They wanted to have an elaborate Mexican dinner, as they loved the country's cuisine. They all decided on tacos. They added various ingredients such as steak, chicken, and vegetables, and barbecued them to enhance the smoky flavour.

"You know, this taco might even be better than Taco Bell's!" said Victor when they were nearly finished. They packed up after eating their dinner. It was nearing half past seven p.m. now.

"Too early to sleep," Doris said. "I wish we could do something."

"Why don't we look at the map? We'll just make sure we follow the right path to reach the museum tomorrow," Michael said, pulling out Victor's map.

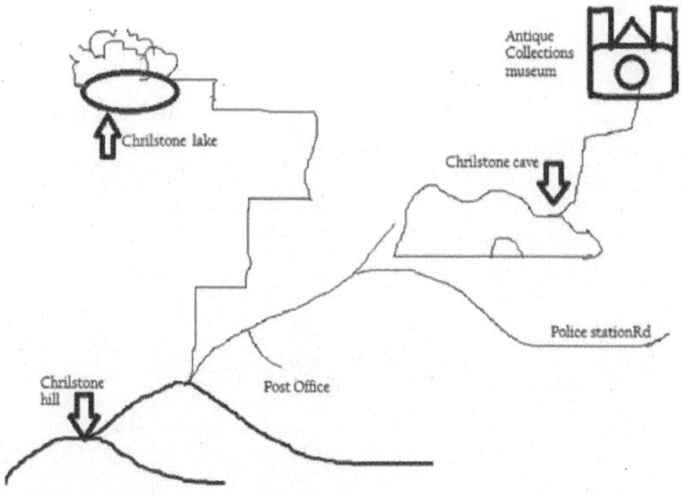

They looked at the directions. Jess noted them down, and after they did so, they all went to eat dinner. Doris started to prepare some quesadillas. They ate their dinner at half past eight. When the smartwatch rang, it was nine o'clock. They brushed their teeth, leapt into their nightdresses, put their feet into flip-flops, and were ready for the night. The night was pitch-black. Crows cawed, owls hooted from afar, a wolf howled in the distance, and the moon was bright and white now.

"Goodnight," the girls said to Michael and Victor. "Have a good night's rest," they said back.

Chapter 6
CYCLING TO THE MUSEUM

Doris was startled awake by someone saying, "Wake up, Doris, wake up!" Still half-asleep and confused, she asked, "What? What is it?"

"It's nine a.m. already! We were supposed to have had breakfast half an hour ago! Don't tell me you forgot about the museum," Michael said.

"Oh, absolutely not," Doris replied. When she finally got up, Jess and Victor had already started eating.

"Thanks for waiting, Michael," Doris said as she joined them.

They were eating muffins, bread and butter, and a side dish of fruit salad, containing strawberries, blueberries, and cherries, drizzled with caramel syrup and honey. They ate quickly because they had to start cycling to the museum soon. Their bicycles were in good condition and did not require pumping. Doris, Victor, Michael, and Jess started cycling, with Jess being the fastest.

After cycling six miles, they decided to rest by a pine tree. Michael complained, "My legs are numb from all that cycling." Suddenly, a large pinecone fell on his head.

"Ouch!" he said. He looked up and saw a squirrel munching on cones, but it slipped one from its hand before disappearing into the thick branches. The group rested quietly.

After a while, they had only two more miles left. They drank water occasionally to keep going. It was nearing noon when they reached the museum. The tall building was surrounded by beige-colored pillars. A huge banner hung on it, showing:

ANTIQUE COLLECTIONS SINCE 1985

The museum looked fabulous and old-fashioned at the same time, giving it a touch of glow and a spark of an eerie sensation.

"Shall we go in?" Doris asked after parking their bicycles in the shade beneath a tree.

"Yes, we shall," Victor replied, and they went in. The museum was silent, with few people inside, because, as you know, not many people lived near or in Chrilstone.

The four came to the paintings. The first one caught Victor's eye.

"Abstract art isn't my style. You know, I've never understood the hidden meaning behind abstract art, but this one doesn't seem bad," Victor said. The picture was of the two sides of life. The painting not only attracted Victor's attention but also sparked an interest in Doris as well.

"Who's the artist?" Jess asked, curious. Her fingerprints were traced to the corner of the painting. The name of the artist was so small, so tiny, that no one could make out who painted this masterpiece.

However, they approached a bronze figurine later. There

was another figurine from the UK called the Willow Tree.

"India always fascinates me. It contains great history about wars like the freedom fight in 1947, dynasties, kingdoms, and much more," Doris said. She knew a lot of general history, indeed.

As they went on, they saw more paintings, and the setting and interior of the rooms started to change gradually. The room they were in had a huge chandelier at the centre of the ceiling. In that room were displays of paintings of the French Revolution and the lives of ordinary French people. It also contained the Arc de Triomphe, which honoured the soldiers who fought for the country's freedom and equality. They were coming to the end of the museum; there were just a few paintings left.

"Time passed quickly, didn't it?" Jess asked.

"Yes, it did. We spent a couple of hours here, gazing at all these amazing paintings," said Michael.

In a few minutes, they completed the tour around the whole museum and went back. They could write their reviews on a sheet of paper, and the four did so. They were the last to leave.

They left the museum and rode back to their tents. On their way, as usual, they passed the butterfly garden and Pedro. Victor waved and shouted, "Pedro! Good to see you again! Where were you a few days ago?"

"Oh, about that… Well, I was just travelling somewhere quite important," Pedro said, stuttering.

"Well, alright. We're going to our tents now," said Jess.

"Bye!" said Pedro, going inside his and his old grandfather's house.

The four of them continued cycling, brushing their fingertips against the beautiful flowers swaying in the breeze. They finally saw their tents in front of them, parked their bicycles, and went inside their respective tents. They were quite hungry.

They unpacked some food from their bags to eat. Michael and Victor unzipped part of their tent. It was sunny, and the shadow of their tent was cast on the ground. Staring at the beautiful surroundings, they munched away.

Hardly had they finished their lunch, they got bored with nothing to do but talk.

"Remember how we pranked our professor last term?"

"That was jolly fun!" Victor said.

They remembered hiding behind curtains and giving their teacher, Mrs Lee, a shock.

"How fun it was to see her books drop down on the floor," Jess said.

"We did get some scoldings, though," Victor said, laughing at the frown on Mrs Lee's face.

"Oh, and that time Mrs Lee got us back by saying we failed the midterm exam! I thought it would be the end of us," Michael said.

"One thing I'll never forget is the first day of high school last year, though I only entered then. We had a class party where everyone bought candies and gummy bears, so we made a candy salad," Doris said.

"And we can't forget our journey to London, where we saw The Thames, Big Ben, and went on a double- decker bus," said Jess.

"Yes, I remember that like the back of my hand," said Michael.

They went on talking until evening. They decided to go on a bicycle ride over the nearby hills as a late evening ride. So they all jumped on their cycles and hurriedly sped down the hill.

The sky was a light rose colour, blending with light orange. The soft hills seemed to stretch on forever.

"Who could have thought Chrilstone was such a beautiful countryside? I wonder why there aren't any tourists interested in exploring Chrilstone's views," Doris said.

"Just look at the terrace farming on the hills and the dewdrops on every plant. It feels like a dream," said Jess.

"It's been a while since I've read the newspaper, but there's only a post office here—what a pity!" said Victor.

"I would love to play the Sudoku games and crosswords on it," Michael said with a sigh. They went on cycling.

"Why don't we head back? The sky's getting grey," said Victor, and so they turned to return to their cosy tents. They were going to eat dinner soon. They reached the tents. The four were equally hungry and unpacked a huge stack of dinner, enough to fill their stomachs. They finished swiftly and had a drink after.

They leapt into their sleeping bags soon after, ready to sleep in their respective tents. As mentioned earlier, the boys slept in one tent, while the girls slept in another.

"I don't want anyone to interrupt my sleep," Doris said. It was certain that the four would never forget their experiences on this trip!

And that time, when all of them were in deep sleep, was when the heist started. It was now half past eleven.

Chapter 7
WHAT'S GOING ON ?????

It was just an ordinary day in November—or so it seemed—when a strong, strange noise erupted out of nowhere, seemingly from underground. Doris woke up startled as the ground rumbled slightly. She unzipped the tent she shared with Jess, stepped outside, and spotted a trail of muddy footprints leading somewhere. Following it, she discovered a round metal lid with a handle right next to the prohibited area they had seen on Chrilstone Hill. Her heart thumped with doubt and excitement; she wondered if the passage led beneath the restricted zone, which was still illegal to enter.

"Looks like someone forgot to lock it," she said, peeking into the deep tunnel revealed when she pried it open. Debating whether to wait for the others due to the danger, Jess woke up, noticed the open tent, and found Doris staring at the hole.

"Doris? What are you doing here?"

"Oh, Jess, well… I was just looking at this odd metal lid that leads to a tunnel."

"A tunnel?" Jess approached the peculiar underground passage. "Under the prohibited area," she mumbled. "Why is it here, and why did we only notice now?"

"I don't know what to do, but it's worth finding out what hides in this long tunnel," Doris replied.

"Alright, let me wake the others while you process what we just uncovered."

Soon, Michael and Victor emerged from their tent, rubbing their eyes, and saw Jess near the hole.

"So, Jess, is this the passage Doris was talking about?" Michael inquired.

"Yes. I was wondering if we could go in. There's a ladder anyway," she said.

"Are you sure we won't get hungry on the way?" Victor asked.

"Maybe I'll take food, just in case," Doris said.

She took a fruit basket and filled it with a container of cut fruits. She also took some toast and water bottles.

She shoved a candy into each of her siblings' pockets.

"Here you go," she said.

Looking back into the passage they had recently discovered, they saw a ladder to climb down.

"It's possible that someone could be down here. I don't think we should go too far," Michael stated.

He went first, then Jess, Doris, and lastly Victor. They shone their torches at the dark, eerie walls that echoed when they spoke. At a distance, they heard a dog barking. The four froze.

"Well, looks like we're not the only ones here," Doris said as they moved further.

"It seems the moment we've waited for has arrived," said

Victor. "My questions are: What was this passage made for? Or maybe we might find someone we know creeping in the dark here." This sent a shiver down everyone's spine. But Victor wasn't wrong—they'd meet the most unexpected person at the worst time. Who could guess who it was? What about a traitor?

As the four continued, their legs grew tired. They sat down.

"Do you think coming down here was a good idea?" Jess asked.

"I mean, we would have a high chance of spotting a mystery here," Michael said. He wouldn't stop pretending to be a detective and talking about mysteries. They went on walking until they came to a dead end. When the four turned to the side, they saw another metal lid above them, with a ladder leading up. "What a complicated path," Victor said, climbing the ladder and trying to turn the handle to open the lid.

"If this doesn't open, we're done for," Doris said. Thankfully, to their relief, the metal lid was easy to open. They popped their heads out. They were not prepared to see what happened next.

"Chrilstone cave?" Jess said in awe. "The tunnel leads here?" She asked, seeing the cave they had visited earlier right in front of them.

"There's no doubt someone must have drilled this tunnel and entered this cave for a reason or purpose," Victor said.

"Or the tunnel could have existed from the beginning, and

maybe we didn't notice it because bushes and grass covered the lid," Michael added. They both had valid points.

"Why don't we go in? Though we've already been here," Michael suggested, unwrapping a candy from his pocket. They all followed him inside.

Soon, they came to the metal door they had noticed before.

"Why don't we check if the door still budges?" Doris suggested.

Jess opened the door, only to find three people—one familiar to her—standing in a circle holding a black box that seemed familiar to her. Startled, she stepped back and squinted to identify the familiar figure.

"Pedro?" she stuttered, spellbound to see her new friend participating in something she never expected.

There were two more people with him, equally stunned by the four's presence. Victor stepped forward to confront Pedro.

"Pedro, what are you doing here?" he demanded.

Pedro remained cool and silent.

Now seven people stood still in the room. Pedro changed; he wasn't the nice Pedro the four had known. Without a word, one of Pedro's acquaintances kicked the door open and rushed out. Before the four could chase, Pedro shut the door.

Victor tried to push it back in vain. The four, expecting an exciting, mysterious time together, were now locked in a room with nearly no way out.

"Let's see how you get out now," Pedro's voice echoed back. The four were not ones to give up easily—if Pedro and his so-called friends thought they had won, they were wrong.

Victor sat down in the empty, dark room.

"A friend so nice at first, that we never thought we'd end up like this," he said.

That's when not only Victor but the other three learned their lesson: someone kind at first might one day be exposed as a ravenous wolf.

"How can we break open a metal door?" Victor asked, starting to lose hope. He placed his head against the door to check if Pedro and the others had left. He spotted a drill nearby.

"Pedro and the other two must have dug the passage with this drill," he said.

He took the drill and started drilling a small hole. It grew larger until it was big enough to climb through.

"Good," Jess said. "We can try all possible ways to get out

now."

"I feel hungry," Doris burst out.

The others stared at her in surprise—what a thing to say at the wrong time! Michael peeked through the hole. To everyone's relief, he saw nobody and stepped out. The others followed, remembering the path back to the entrance and fresh daylight. They had had enough of the dark.

"We're out of the cave!" Doris exclaimed.

"But wait, where could Pedro have gone?" Victor asked.

"I totally forgot about that. But I suggest we go back to our tents, and we'll find an explanation for all this," Jess said.

"You may be right—what if Pedro and his friends return?" said Michael. They all headed back.

The four siblings silently finished their breakfast, still in awe of the day's events. Well, at least they got what they wanted—a mystery. But it wasn't fully solved yet. What was in that black chest Pedro held? The answer to the mystery relied on that. Not sure about re-entering the cave, they went to fifteen-year-old Pedro's house with the butterfly garden alongside it. On their bicycles, they reached it. They were about to ring the doorbell, frightened, not knowing who would answer. Their hearts thumped.

"An open window!" Doris said. "Let me see through it to know who's inside." Thankfully, they only spotted the old man baking in his kitchen. He was the only person on the ground floor. Ding dong! The four rang the doorbell.

Gladly, it was the old man who answered.

"Oh, dear children, long time no see!" he said. The four greeted him and cautiously walked inside.

"Has Pedro by any chance come here?" Victor asked.

"Oh yes, he came with a black box and headed to his bedroom, but in a few minutes, he left the house," the old man said.

The five climbed the stairs when the old man went to water his garden.

"Where could the box be?" Victor thought. He bent down to look under the bed and he finally found it! He blew off the dust and opened it.

"Jade stone?" he exclaimed, surprised. "Is it real?" "But where did Pedro get this from?" Michael asked.

Doris was just as shocked as her siblings.

As they talked, they heard the door open. The old man was talking to someone; the four couldn't recognise who at first until they peeped through the door. It was Pedro, introducing his two friends: James and Arthur.

"Quick, let's hide!" said Doris, afraid they might get caught.

They heard footsteps growing louder on each step, so the four kept the case back and hid in the closet. They overheard everything Pedro, James, and Arthur said.

"There's no way anyone is going to find out," came Pedro's voice. "But I'm still wondering how my four friends escaped."

"You still call them your friends?" Arthur asked. "Well,

oh, I meant enemies. Yes! Enemies, sorry though," said Pedro. This broke the siblings' hearts.

"Anyways, I'm going to the bathroom. You both can stay here till one o'clock—that's in about two hours," Pedro said. James and Arthur went for a short snooze. "Now's our chance," Jess said. They'd had enough of overhearing the awful things Pedro and the two said. The four crept out of the room very quietly, went downstairs, opened the front door, and started running for their lives. They panted. At least they weren't caught.

Chapter 8
THE MYSTERY IS SOLVED

The first thing they did was telephone the police. What a relief to have a police station nearby— it would be convenient, even though the area was scantily populated. They reported the stolen jade stone, which could have been dug up from the prohibited area by accessing it through the passage they found. The officers were on their way. They needed to be quick because Pedro, Arthur, and James would only be in the old man's house till 1 o'clock. But yes, just as they expected, the cops arrived early. The four had been waiting desperately. They showed the way to the old man's house. The police knocked. The old man opened the door and turned pale. He was terrified because he thought he was going to get arrested.

"Don't worry, sir. Would Pedro, James, and Arthur be free at the moment?" one officer asked.

"I don't understand," the old man said. He called the three downstairs anyway. Pedro, James, and Arthur went white instantly when they saw the police—and most importantly, the four siblings along with them. They knew it was the end.

"Wait," Pedro tried saying. "It's not what you think!"

"We'll be taking these three for questioning, sir.

Thank you for your patience. We'll be back in a jiffy."

The five waited until the questioning was finished. The culprits confessed that they had committed the crime for money.

The police saw the crystals in the box and confirmed that they were real. After the questioning was done, the police collected all the necessary information to tell the four.

"So, jumping to conclusions, we befriended a traitor who discovered a passage that would lead to the prohibited area and further to the cave. Pedro and his two friends explored the prohibited area only to discover a jade stone there and hide it in the cave. The worst part is that it was a restricted area accessible only to the government. The three were planning to sell these in another state at an opportune time," Jess said.

"But gladly, the police will be taking the initiative and the responsibility to question them for a few more days, until the final decision is made."

They headed back to the tents, happy and satisfied that they stood against Pedro for the right reason. "Pity it's our last day here," Doris said, after they finished packing and jumped on their bicycles. The others agreed. They had the best moment of their lifetime ever! What would their parents think?

"I think they'd be proud that we solved a mystery— well, of course, with the help of others too," Doris said. Well, they had a really long story to tell their parents.

For now, bye, you four! Let's cross our fingers for more mysteries for you to solve.

THE END

Sarah Bijo Johns

Sarah is a passionate girl who focuses on her reading and writing skills, while maintaining time for her hobby: singing. She is fun, and her favorite genre is mystery. That's why she wrote this book. The main characters are kind and loyal, and they are inspired by her friends and family. Hope you'll enjoy this book!